THE TALE OF THE FLOPSY BUNNIES AND MRS TITTLEMOUSE

From the authorized animated series
based on the original tales
^{TM}
BY **BEATRIX POTTER**

F. WARNE & Co.

It is said that the effect of eating too much lettuce is "soporific."
I have never felt sleepy after eating lettuces; but then I am not a rabbit.
They certainly had a very soporific effect upon the Flopsy Bunnies!
  When Benjamin Bunny grew up, he married his Cousin Flopsy.
They had a large family, and they were very improvident and cheerful.
I do not remember the separate names of their children; they were
generally called the "Flopsy Bunnies".

As there was not always quite enough to eat, Benjamin used to borrow cabbages from Flopsy's brother, Peter Rabbit, who kept a nursery garden.

Sometimes Peter Rabbit had no cabbages to spare. When this happened, the Flopsy Bunnies went across the field to a rubbish heap, in the ditch outside Mr McGregor's garden.

Mr McGregor's rubbish heap was a mixture. There were jam pots and paper bags, and some rotten vegetable marrows and an old boot or two. One day – oh joy! – there were a quantity of overgrown lettuces.

A little wood-mouse was picking over the rubbish among the jam pots. Her name was Mrs Tittlemouse.

"Good afternoon, Ma'am," said Benjamin Bunny. "Pray excuse my youngsters – they have waited overlong for their lunch today!"

"Then I think I shall go home," said Mrs Tittlemouse, "before I am eaten in mistake for a lettuce!"

Mrs Tittlemouse lived alone in a bank under a hedge. Such a funny house!

There were yards and yards of sandy passages, leading to storerooms and nut and seed cellars.

There was a kitchen, a parlour, a pantry, and a larder. Also, there was Mrs Tittlemouse's bedroom, where she slept in a little box bed!

Mrs Tittlemouse was a most terribly particular little mouse, always sweeping and dusting the soft sandy floors.

Sometimes a beetle lost its way in the passages. "Shuh! shuh! little dirty feet!" said Mrs Tittlemouse, clattering her dust-pan.

And one day a little old woman ran up and down in a red spotty cloak. "Your house is on fire, Mother Ladybird! Fly away home to your children!"

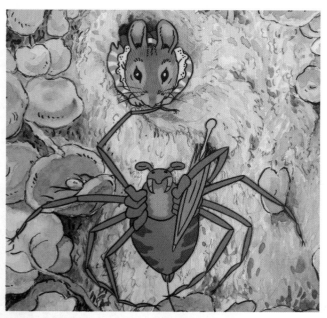

Another day, a big fat spider came in to shelter from the rain. "Beg pardon, is this not Miss Muffet's?" "Go away, you bold bad spider! Leaving ends of cobweb all over my nice clean house!" Mrs Tittlemouse bundled the spider out at a window.

It was dinner time. "I shall go to my furthest storeroom and fetch cherry stones and thistle-down seed..." said Mrs Tittlemouse. Suddenly round a corner, she met Babbitty Bumble. "Zizz, Bizz, Bizz!" said the bumble bee, in a peevish squeak, and she sidled down a side passage.

Three or four other bees buzzed fiercely. "I am not in the habit of letting lodgings; this is an intrusion!" said Mrs Tittlemouse crossly. "I will have them turned out! I wonder who would help me? . . . Mr Benjamin Bunny, of course! Benjamin Bunny will help me drive out these tiresome bees!"

7

Mrs Tittlemouse went back to the rubbish heap.

The Flopsy Bunnies had simply stuffed lettuces and by degrees, one after another, they had been overcome with slumber.

Benjamin was not so much overcome as his children. Before going to sleep he was sufficiently wide awake to put a paper bag over his head to keep off the flies. The little Flopsy Bunnies slept delightfully in the warm sun.

Mrs Tittle-mouse rustled across the paper bag, and awakened Benjamin Bunny.

"Mr Benjamin, I am so sorry to disturb you, but as we are both acquainted with Mr Peter Rabbit I thought to ask a favour of you... oh Mr Benjamin, I am having such trouble with *bees* in my house!"

"Bees, yes, indeed Ma'am, very tiresome creatures," said Benjamin sleepily.

A robin arrived with a whir of wings and a flash of red. "Oh, Mr Red-breast!" said Mrs Tittlemouse, "could *you* help me with my nest of bees?"

Then they heard a heavy tread above their heads. Mr McGregor was approaching. "The Flopsy Bunnies! Mr McGregor is sure to see the Flopsy Bunnies," said Mrs Tittlemouse. "We must wake them up, we must warn them!" But it was impossible to wake the Flopsy Bunnies.

The robin darted around Mr
McGregor's head, trying to distract
him. Suddenly, he emptied out a
sackful of lawn mowings right upon
the top of the sleeping Flopsy Bunnies!
Benjamin shrank down under his paper bag.
Mrs Tittlemouse hid in a jam pot.

The little rabbits smiled sweetly in
their sleep under the shower of
grass. Mr McGregor looked down.
He saw some funny little brown
tips of ears sticking up through
the lawn mowings. He stared
at them for some time.

Presently a fly settled on one of them and it moved. Mr McGregor climbed down on to the rubbish heap – "One, two, three, four! five! six leetle rabbits!" said he as he dropped them into his sack.

Mr McGregor tied up the sack and left it on the wall. He went to put away the mowing machine.

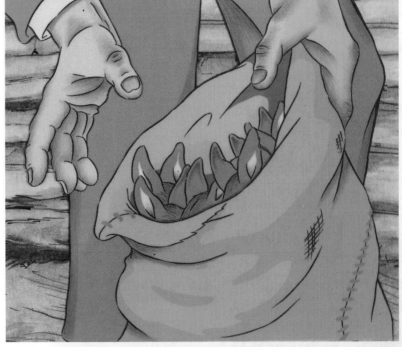

Then Mrs Tittlemouse came out of her jam pot, and Benjamin took the paper bag off his head. They could see the sack, up on the wall.
Just then Mrs Flopsy Bunny (who had remained at home) came across the field.

She looked suspiciously at the sack and wondered where everybody was? "Mr McGregor has caught your babies and put them in this sack!" said Mrs Tittlemouse.

Benjamin and Flopsy were in despair; they could not undo the string.

"My poor babies, what shall we do?" said Flopsy. But Mrs Tittlemouse was a resourceful person. "Why, Mrs Tittlemouse, whatever can you be doing?" said Benjamin. She was nibbling a hole in the bottom corner of the sack!

The little rabbits were pulled out and pinched to wake them.

Their parents stuffed the empty
sack with three rotten vegetable
marrows, an old blacking-
brush and two decayed
turnips.

"We'll see what old
McGregor thinks about
that!" said Benjamin, and
they all hid under a bush
and watched for him.

Mrs Tittlemouse hastily
said good day and went home.

Mr McGregor had come back to fetch the sack. He carried it off carefully, for he believed the Flopsy Bunnies were still sleeping peacefully inside, but if he had looked behind he would have seen them following at a safe distance!

They watched him go into his house, and then they crept up to the window to listen.

16

Mr McGregor threw down the sack on the stone floor. "One, two, three, four, five, six leetle rabbits!" said Mr McGregor.
(The youngest Flopsy Bunny got upon the window-sill.)

Mrs McGregor took hold of the sack and felt it. She untied the sack and put her hand inside. When she felt the vegetables she became very very angry.

A rotten marrow came flying through the kitchen window, and hit the youngest Flopsy Bunny. It was rather hurt.

Then Benjamin and Flopsy thought it was time to go home.

What a surprise awaited Mrs Tittlemouse on her return home! When she got back to the parlour, she heard some one coughing in a fat voice, and there sat Mr Jackson! "How do you do, Mr Jackson? Deary me, you have got very wet feet!" said Mrs Tittlemouse. "Thank you, thank you, thank you, Mrs Tittlemouse! I'll sit awhile and dry myself," said Mr Jackson. He sat and smiled, and the water dripped off his coat tails. Mrs Tittlemouse went round with a mop.

He sat such a while that he had to be asked if he would take some dinner? First she offered him some cherry stones. "No teeth, no teeth, no teeth!" mumbled Mr Jackson, opening his mouth unnecessarily wide; he certainly had not a tooth in his head.

"Thistledown seed, Mr Jackson?" "Tiddly, widdly, widdly! Pouff, pouff, puff!" said Mr Jackson. He blew the thistledown all over the room.

"Thank you, thank you, thank you, Mrs Tittlemouse, but what I really – *really* should like – would be a dish of honey! I can smell it, that's why I came to call." He rose ponderously from the table, and began to look into the cupboards. Mrs Tittlemouse followed with a dish-cloth.

Mr Jackson began to walk down the passage. "Indeed, indeed, you will stick fast, Mr Jackson!" said Mrs Tittlemouse. They went along the sandy passage – "Tiddly widdly –"

"Buzz! Wizz! Wizz!" He met Babbitty round a corner, and snapped her up, and put her down again. "I do not like bumble bees, they are all over bristles," said Mr Jackson, wiping his mouth with his coat sleeve.

"Get out, you nasty old toad!" shrieked Babbitty Bumble. "I shall go distracted!" scolded Mrs Tittlemouse.

Mr Jackson pulled out the bees nest and ate the honey. He seemed to have no objection to stings. The bees gathered up their pollen-bags and flew away, down the passages and out of the windows and doors of the little house, and away over the fields, to find a quieter place for their nest. Mrs Tittlemouse shut herself in the nut cellar.

When Mrs Tittlemouse ventured out of the nut cellar, everybody had gone away. But the untidiness was something dreadful. She went out and fetched some twigs, to partly close up the front door. "I will make it too small for Mr Jackson!"

But she was too tired to do any more. First she fell asleep in her chair, and then she went to bed. "Will it ever be tidy again?" said poor Mrs Tittlemouse.

Next morning she got up very early and did a spring cleaning which lasted a fortnight.

When it was all beautifully neat and clean, she gave a party to five other mice, without Mr Jackson. He smelt the party and came up the bank, but he could not squeeze in at the door. Mrs Tittlemouse had quite forgiven him, and although she had no food to suit his taste, she handed him out acorn-cupfuls of honey-dew through the window, and he was not at all offended.

The flopsy Bunnies did not forget Mrs Tittlemouse.
Next Christmas Thomasina Tittlemouse got a present of
enough rabbit-wool to make herself a cloak and a hood,
and a handsome muff and a pair of warm mittens.

THE END